FLYNTLOCK BONES

THE EYE OF MOGDROD

By Derek Keilty

Illustrated by Mark Elvins

Scallywag Press Ltd
LONDON

Dire Straits

Mystic Sea

Bohemia

The Seven Seas

Cutlass Sea

Shark Sea

Calcutlass Island

Sharktooth Island

GALLERY of CHARACTERS

The Crew of The Black Hound

Flynn

Red

Cap'n Watkins

Briggs

Arthur

Hudson

Scratch

The Twins

Fishbreath

The Rest

Chief Fergus McSwaggers

Mog drod

Egfart

Grethel

Ice Captain

Squabbler Swamp

Plunderer's Peat

Bog Island

Skulleen Abbey

Skulleen

Lake Squelch

Mugger's Marsh

Bog Village

Bog Castle

Bogland Bay

Swampy Bog

Craggy Hills

Grethel's Lighthouse

CHAPTER ONE
THE PARROT

Thwack! Bump! crash!

My hammock tips over and I land on the floor of the ship's sleeping quarters with an almighty thud. Red, the ship's rigger, is bellowing in my ear.

'Time to get up!' she yells. 'Call yerself Flyntlock Bones, I'd say more like Lazy Bones! The Black Hound don't sail itself, y'know.'

1

I sit up and rub my head, still in a drowsy fog.

'Don't you ever sleep in?' I complain. 'What time is it?'

'Early. Sun en't even up yet.'

I struggle to my feet. Red can be so annoying, but perhaps she's done me a favour this time.

'Actually, I'm glad you woke me,' I admit. 'I was having the weirdest dream. I was back at the orphanage in Baskervile and Mrs Wiggins, the old matron, had a long bushy beard and was waving a cutlass about. She was laughing and swigging on a bottle of grog, just like an old pirate.'

Red grins.
'Sounds like
a nightmare.'

Along with the
rest of the crew of the
Black Hound, Red and
I might look like pirates,
but there's more to us than meets the eye.
In fact, we are ex-pirates turned detectives,
or 'pirate investigators' as we like to call
ourselves. Now we sail the Seven Seas finding
stolen booty for anyone who chooses to hire
us. Last year, Captain Watkins gave me a
week's trial as cabin boy, and although I was
a mere landlubber who'd only ever lived in
an orphanage, I am happy to say I passed with
flying colours. I have never looked back.

3

I follow Red up on deck to stare at the faint twinkles of stars and the hint of light on the horizon where the sun will soon rise. Around the ship, the sea stretches for miles in every direction with not a glimpse of land to be seen.

'Where are we?' I ask.

Looking up at the sky, Red ponders for a moment.

'Well, that's Orion, one of the constellations.'

'What's a constellation?'

'It's an imaginary pattern, like a person or an animal, that's made up by stars. Orion is one of 'em, in the shape of an ol' hunter. A good bosun like our Hudson can navigate just by lookin' at the stars.' She points at the brightest star in the sky. 'But so can I. Look up there, that's the Alpha star. It shines brighter than all the others, so by my reckoning, we must be in the Bellgravyan Sea.'

I gasp, impressed. 'You can tell all that by the stars?'

'I'm joking,' she chuckles. 'I haven't the foggiest idea where we are. C'mon.' And she disappears below the hatch, laughing.

Down in the galley, Fishbreath, the ship's cook, is busily preparing breakfast. He's the proud owner of the droopiest moustache in all the Seven Seas, not to mention a missing hand. But he doesn't have a hook like most pirates – instead he has a large silver spoon, which comes in pretty useful for a cook. And he has an enormous pet parrot on his shoulder, called Arthur.

This morning, Fishbreath seems a bit grouchy, with not so much as a 'Good morning,' or even a grunt for a greeting. He ladles some gruel from an old battered pot into a bowl, which I examine to pick out floating weevils. I stopped asking what was in the food months ago, as Red says it's sometimes best not to know the ingredients Fishbreath uses to make the ship's grub.

'What's the matter, Fishbreath?' I ask.

He groans. 'Just had some of the crew grumblin' in me ear about rations. They said now we're one man down aboard ship, they should get more food, 'cause they 'ave to do more work.'

I am not sure getting bigger portions of Fishbreath's food is a very good idea.

'What did you say?'

'Told them to quit gripin'. Now Drudger's gone, it's all shoulders to the wheel.'

I prefer not to think about Drudger. He used to work as a rigger on the Hound, but he was a bully, and worse still he let the Captain down badly the first chance he got. I am glad he isn't about anymore, but it does mean there are a lot more chores to do round the ship now.

'Yez should be thankful ya got time to eat,' Fishbreath goes on. 'I heard the Captain's thinking about making us all work through our meals.'

Red nudges me. 'That's why we're taking ours away with us.'

Scratch, the ship's cat, wanders by looking for some scraps, and I give her a rub behind the ears. I'm pretty sure that if Scratch could hoist the sails, then the Captain would have her working at that too.

9

As we get up to leave, Captain Watkins strides into the galley, almost bowling us over. He is wearing a three-cornered hat, a long coat and a ruffled shirt. A cutlass hangs off the belt that holds up his smart velvet trousers. And his sharp nose looks just like a beak.

'Ah, there you are,' he says. 'I've been looking for you two.'

He gives Red and me a cheery smile, putting a match to his pipe, puffing and blowing.

'We've been up before sunrise, Cap'n Watkins,' says Red. 'You won't catch us snoozing in our hammocks, not when there's work to be done.' She elbows me.

'Aye, she's right there, Cap'n,' I add, glaring at her.

The Captain says, 'Look, I realise it's all-hands-on-deck just now, but I have a plan to get us back to normal again. Back in my pirating days, recruiting a new shipmate was as easy as tossing a hood over some dozy landlubber and dragging him aboard whether he liked it or not.' He pauses. 'But times have changed,' he adds.

Grinning at our gaping mouths, he takes a pile of blank cards and a pen from his coat pocket. 'Flynn will recall I've got a different way of adding to the crew – that's how he came to join us himself. So Flynn and Red, I want you

to write me out some job advertising cards.
Something like:

Rigger Wanted
for the Black Hound
apply at Bellgravya Harbour

Do about fifty of 'em each, and quick as you
can. Won't be long till we dock at Bellgravya,
then you can go ashore and leave them in the
shops around town.'

Red's eyes dart between me and the Captain.
'Er, I've the rig to set, then lookout duty, Cap'n,
and we'll need to keep our eyes peeled…'

For some reason she is making excuses, and
the Captain isn't fooled.

'Take them up with you to the crow's nest.
You can make a start from up there.'

'Aye, sir.' Red looks downcast. I wonder why,

as there are much worse jobs than writing out cards to do aboard the Hound, like mopping up sick after one of Fishbreath's dodgy meals and a choppy night.

When the Captain leaves, we head for the main mast. I can see Red still isn't too sure.

'I'll do your chores, if you'll do the cards, Flynn,' she offers.

'Don't you want to write the cards?'

I notice Red's cheeks glow pink and her eyes drop. 'It's just, well, truth be told, I never learned to read or write. Couldn't see the point.'

'I see. Well, nothin' to be worried about. I could teach you.'

'Thanks, but I don't think I could ever do it...'

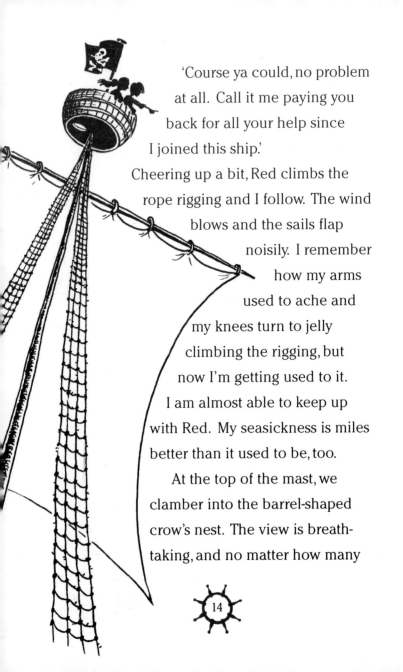

'Course ya could, no problem at all. Call it me paying you back for all your help since I joined this ship.'

Cheering up a bit, Red climbs the rope rigging and I follow. The wind blows and the sails flap noisily. I remember how my arms used to ache and my knees turn to jelly climbing the rigging, but now I'm getting used to it. I am almost able to keep up with Red. My seasickness is miles better than it used to be, too.

At the top of the mast, we clamber into the barrel-shaped crow's nest. The view is breath-taking, and no matter how many times I climb up there, I always stop for a moment to take it in, sucking in a big breath of salty sea air.

We sit in the barrel, where we are sheltered from the wind.

'Once I get a few cards written, I'll start by teaching you the alphabet and the sounds the letters make,' I say.

'I can't,' Red protests.

'Yes, you can.'

SQUAWK!

Red stands up as I hear a flutter of wings.

'Now we can't. There en't gonna be time for all that. Look.'

'A parrot!' I say.

'Aye, but look, there's a note tied to its leg. An' you know what that means?'

My heart flutters faster than the parrot's wings.

'The next case for the pirate investigators!' I gasp.

CHAPTER TWO
THE STOLEN BOOTY

The parrot perches on the edge of the crow's nest.

'Should call it the parrot's nest!' I joke. I watch Red carefully untying the string that secures the note to the parrot's spindly leg. Taking the note, she gives the messenger a treat from her pocket, then it flies off.

'C'mon, we got to get this to the Captain, and sharpish.'

'Is it a new case?' I ask eagerly. 'Can I have a look?'

'Captain don't like anyone seeing it before him. He says he can tell if the scroll has been opened.'

I'm busting to know what the note says. I think back to my first case, and Miss Wrinkly's plea for help over the museum robbery that had us setting sail for the Great Pyramids of the Gypshun Sea. Who was in trouble this time? What part of the Seven Seas would we be exploring next? The life of a pirate investigator was always so exciting.

I follow Red down the rigging to the helm, where she hands the note to Captain Watkins.

'This just arrived by parrot, Cap'n.'

'Splendid. Good job, Red.' He unrolls the note, reads it, then rolls it up again. 'Have you made a start on those job cards?' he asks.

I shake my head. 'We were about to when the parrot arrived.'

'Well, I wouldn't bother, as this note changes everything. We won't be going to Bellgravya after all.'

Briggs, the first mate, a big, burly man with an eye patch and thick bushy beard, overhears this as he passes by.

'Change o' plan, Cap'n? What's happened?' he asks.

Watkins hands him the note.

'Got us a new case, Briggs. Could be a tough one too, by the sounds of it. Reckon we'll need our wits about us.'

The Captain calls out for Hudson, the ship's bosun.

'Bring her about, Master Hudson, and set a course for the Frozen Sea.'

Hudson, a barrel-shaped sailor with short, stubby legs, is the one in charge of everything that keeps us afloat and heading the right way. He looks alarmed.

'The Frozen Sea, Cap'n? But...'

'No buts, Hudson,' interrupts Watkins. 'An' inform the rest of the crew, I want yez all in my cabin, and sharpish.' The bosun scuttles off obediently, and Captain Watkins strides away.

The Captain's cabin is large and gloomy, with one tiny window letting in a thin shaft of light.

The desk is cluttered with candles, maps and a magnifying glass. In the corner, a grinning skeleton is holding a violin, and a packed bookcase runs along the far wall.

The crew arrive one by one and cluster round
the desk, sitting on barrels or on the hard,
wooden floor. Hudson is last, and the Captain
waits for him to join us before announcing the
arrival of the new note. He reads it aloud, in
his best Piratish:

Ahoy, yez miserable scurvy bilge rats! My name is Fergus McSwaggers, chief of the Bog Barbarian clan in the Boglands. Some treacherous, flea-bitten, lily-livered scallywag has gone an' stolen me most precious piece of booty, a priceless golden chalice. Plundered it from the tower of me castle in the dead o' night, and I be needin' yer help to get it back. The Boglands be the perfect place for us landlubbers, though it's as damp as a dog's nose, and misty all year round. It's a rapscallion of a place to find anything in this foul fog, let alone pilfered treasure. But I hear if there's anyone who can find stolen booty, then it be the loot-locating buccaneers o' the famous Black Hound.

Fergus McSwaggers

P.S. I've drawn a map o' the Boglands and my castle for yez weevil-eatin' sea dogs, so that should show the way here.

No sooner has the Captain finished when Fishbreath leaps off his barrel, his face paler than a snowman's ghost.

'You're not seriously thinking of taking this case on, Cap'n?' he asks.

The rest of the crew stare at him, eyebrows raised. It's not like Fishbreath to be so bold with the boss.

'Why ever not?' replies the Captain, taken aback. 'Seems like the perfect case to get our teeth into.'

Fishbreath gulps, his eyes bulging with what looks like panic. 'Well, for starters the Frozen Sea is crawling with deadly Ice Pirates who'll kill you with their frosty cutlasses as soon as look at yez. And as for those Bogland clans, they're all backstabbin' barbarians. I've heard ya need eyes in the back of yer head to survive even a day on them shores.'

There is a silence while everyone takes this in.

23

'Go on,' says the Captain calmly.

Fishbreath looks around for support, but we are all staring down at our boots.

'Anyways, I thought we was sailing to Bellgravya to get the crew some help? Their hands be torn to ribbons climbing up an' down that rig without a break.'

The Captain smiles.

'I see what you're saying, Fishbreath, but this Fergus McSwaggers doesn't sound like a backstabbing barbarian to me. And he has asked for our help – we can't just ignore that.'

Briggs, the first mate, bangs his fist on the table. 'And it en't like the crow's nest is crammed full of parrots with new cases tied to their feet,' he cries.

'Aye, beggars can't be choosers,' agrees Hudson. 'We need the work. We can sail for

Bellgravya after this case is over, to recruit a new rigger.'

The Captain strokes his chin and frowns.

'Ya got something against this Fergus McSwaggers, Fishbreath?' he asks. 'I never seen you so dead against taking a case from someone you don't even know!'

'Oh, I know him alright.' Fishbreath stares at his upside-down reflection in the spoon he uses for a hand, breathing a deep sigh. 'Fergus McSwaggers is my brother!'

The cabin is suddenly very quiet. Everyone gawks at Fishbreath.

'Known him ten years an' I didn't even know he had a brother,' whispers Briggs.

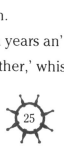

'Your brother!' exclaims the Captain. 'But I don't understand. Surely that's all the more reason for you to try to help him.'

Fishbreath shakes his head. 'Not so, Captain. Ya see, Fergus and I don't exactly hit it off, on account of him bein' the eldest and reelin' in all our pa's inheritance when the old man died. Me, I didn't get a single penny. What does it matter who's the eldest? They're usually the most annoying, bossing all the young 'uns about the place. When we were kids, Fergus was always shoving me around. Then, when he gets

all the loot, he sails up to the Boglands, buys a fancy castle and pretends to be a king. I never even got an invite to come and visit… It's like he forgot all about his brother.'

'Well, he's invited you now,' says the Captain, looking irritated by Fishbreath's moaning. If there is one thing he can't stand, it's a whinger.

Hudson is quick to change the subject.

'Cap'n, I can set us a course that will steer us clear of any perilous Ice Pirates along the way,' he says.

Captain Watkins looks at Red, and the twins, Dedweird and Snitch, who are riggers just like her.

'We'll soon be steering into chilly waters, so you lot will need to be extra careful when ya climb the ropes. It's going to get pretty cold round here, an' I don't want to find any of you hanging from the yard arms, frozen solid like a row of icicles.'

Red swallows hard. 'Aye, Cap'n,' she says.

'That's it then, meeting's over,' Watkins announces. 'Back to yer posts and buckle down for our voyage to the Frozen Sea, and our next case...'

Fishbreath is first to head for the cabin door, slamming it hard behind him.

CHAPTER THREE
THE CASTLE

The bowsprit of the Black Hound cuts through the fog as an icy wind ripples the sails. Despite Fishbreath's protests, the Captain always has the final word. We are now well on our way to the Frozen Sea.

Red and I pull our coats tight round us as we swab the decks.

'Ya ever seen an Ice Pirate, Red?' I ask.

'Not yet I haven't, but I hear they got locks o' ghostly white hair tumbling down their shoulders like a snow drift, and if you touch 'em you get frostbite so bad your hand drops off.'

'You make them sound like monsters.'

'They en't far off it, from what I hear.'

'Land ahoy!' Hudson calls.

Up ahead, a green craggy coastline comes into view, with jagged cliffs, tidal pools and waves crashing on rocks. Following Fergus's map, we sail along the coast until the outline of his castle comes into view. Built on a hilltop which slopes down to the sea, Bog Castle sits proudly, skirted by a swirly mist. It is the first castle I have ever seen that isn't just a picture in a book.

'Wow, look there! That's amazing!' I gasp.

As the Black Hound drops anchor, the Captain gathers us all together.

'Splendid job finding this place in all that fog, Hudson,' he says. 'Now Flynn, Red and Fishbreath,

you'll come ashore with me right now to meet this
Fergus McSwaggers fellow, to find out what his note
is all about.' He holds up the scroll that was flown
in by the parrot. 'The rest of you will stay here
and man the Hound, to watch out for any o' those
sneaky Ice Pirates that lurk around these shores.'

My heart leaps. Although the Captain had
chosen me to help with the last investigation,
there was no guarantee he'd pick me every
time. But I'd been pretty sure he'd take
Fishbreath, on account of Fergus McSwaggers
being his long-lost brother and all that.

Red gives me a nudge. 'Looks like we're on
the case again, Flynn. Reckon the Captain thinks
we're a good team.'

I grin.

'I don't mind staying aboard,'
Fishbreath pipes up. 'Got a
feelin' this might be a long, tough
case, and the crew waiting back
here will need to be fed…'

Nonsense, Fishbreath,' interrupts the
Captain. 'I'm sure they can survive for a day or
two without your culinary delights.' He gives
me a wink. 'Besides I'm sure you're looking
forward to seeing your big brother again after
all these years.'

Fishbreath wrinkles his nose, like he's just
smelled a rotten egg.

'Aye, Cap'n,' he mutters.

As night falls we reach the shore
and start up the hill toward
the castle.

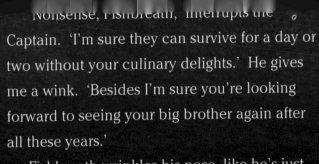

'This is so different to Baskervile,' I say. 'It's so wild, and there are trees everywhere.'

The Captain nods. 'Plenty of places for a thief to hide.'

Suddenly a high-pitched scream comes from somewhere deep in the forest, making me jump out of my skin.

'Did you hear that?' I ask Red.

'What?' she says.

'Like a scream or something.'

'Probably just a bird or wild pig squealing.'

We go on, and as we approach the castle, I notice there are horses and carts tied up outside the old stone walls.

'Looks like we en't the only ones paying your brother a visit,' Captain Watkins says.

Walking round the side of the castle, we peer through a narrow window into the enormous Great Hall. Flaming torches line the walls, casting long shadows on tables and chairs that are arranged in a horseshoe-shape around a roaring fire. Sitting on the chairs are a bunch of big, bearded men and fearsome, hairy women, all wearing dirty, food-spattered woollen tunics.

'That's Fergus at the top of the table dressed in a white robe, playing King o' the Castle,' Fishbreath points out. 'And the rest of the bunch are probably chiefs and leaders of the Bogland villages.'

As we watch, Fergus bangs his drinking horn on the table, calling for order. Then he lifts a gruesome skull in the air. The hairs on my neck stand on end and a chill runs up my spine. Fergus passes the skull along the table to a bulky chief with arms as thick as tree trunks, and a beard like an exploding bird's nest.

'I call on Egfart the Odorous, Chief of the Swamp Squabbler Clan!' Fergus declares.

'Egfart the Odorous!' The name echoes around the hall.

The big chief rises to his feet and, taking the skull, he stomps into the middle of the gathering.

'Not three days ago, a bloodthirsty band of villains came from the coast to raid our village,' Egfart roars, drawing his sword. 'At first, I thought they were Boglanders from the North, but their deathly pale faces and frosty locks told me they had to be vile Ice Pirates.

35

Covered in battle scars they were, but I was
going to give 'em a few more. Aarrgh!'

'Aarrgh!' the Boglanders chorus back,
banging their drinking horns on the table.

'He's telling a story,' I whisper to Red.

'Aye, about Ice Pirates,' Red answers grimly.
'Seems these Boglanders love a good fright.'

Egfart continues his tale once the clamour
has died down.

'The biggest of the Ice Pirates lunges at me,
but with a slash of my sword I send his icicle
flying and him scuttling after it. I look up to
see more of 'em flooding into the village, their
blades flashing in the sun. But those frosty souls
are no match for us scary Swamp Squabblers.

38

Swords clash and in no time at all, we send them scampering back to their frosty white ship, bobbing out in the bay.'

'Aarrgh!' More cheers and horn-cup banging.

I stare at all the food bowls on the table, now empty and licked clean, and imagine them full of roast meat, vegetables and fruit. My belly rumbles. How many more long stories like this will I have to listen to before I get a bite to eat at last? But no such luck.

'Freeze! Don't move a muscle, ya scurvy bunch of Ice Pirates!' growls a gruff voice behind us.

CHAPTER FOUR
THE GREAT FEAST

I spin round to see two burly guards wearing pointy helmets, jabbing their spears at the four of us. They look us up and down, their beady eyes peering out of grubby faces.

'Drop yer weapons!' one shouts. 'Or we'll run yez through!'

'Hold off a moment,' says the other one more quietly, staring at Red. 'They don't look like Ice Pirates to me. You ever seen one with red hair?'

'Aye, you've got a point,' the other admits. 'An' they don't look cold enough either.'

'Well, they're not Boglanders, that's for sure.'

'You're quite right,' cuts in Captain Watkins, his voice a little shaky. 'We're not Ice Pirates or Boglanders. We're pirate investigators!'

'What in the name of thunder is a pirate investigator?' exclaims the guard.

'And more to the point, what are you doing poking around our castle?' demands his friend.

'We're here to visit Fergus McSwaggers, Chief of the Bog Barbarians,' explains the Captain, offering the note. 'He sent us this message by parrot.'

The guard snatches the note out of the Captain's hand and begins to read. Then he grunts. 'Reckon a pirate wrote this.'

'An Ice Pirate!' The other one growls.

I roll my eyes. It is time to clear up the confusion.

'Well, I can assure you we are not Ice Pirates, and maybe if you show Chief McSwaggers this note, he will confirm that I am telling the truth.'

The guards poke spears in our backs and march us inside the tall arched entrance, down a long gloomy corridor and into the Great Hall. As we are pushed inside, the storytelling, bowl banging and cheering all comes to an abrupt halt. The hall is deathly quiet.

'Found this lot creepin' about outside, Chief,' the guard announces.

Fergus leaps off his throne. 'Captain Watkins. It's an honour. I can't believe it, you actually came! You got my parrot then?'

'Yes, I did, and of course I came. Pleased to meet you, Chief McSwaggers.'

'Oh please, call me Fergus. No call for pomp and ceremony here in the Boglands. Well now,

this is a perfect end to a great night's feasting.
I only wish you'd been here earlier, as there
would have been a lot more grub for you to
scoff, but don't worry, I'll make sure both you
and yer men are well looked after, aarrgh!'

I am pretty sure he is doing the annoying
'aarrgh' thing just cos he thinks that's how
we speak.

Red pushes Fishbreath forward and he
stumbles out of the shadows. The Captain laughs.

'I have a surprise for you, Fergus.
Remember your brother, Fishbreath? He's one
of my crew, and he's come to see you too.'

Fergus stares at Fishbreath, tilting his head from side to side like the Captain does when he is examining a footprint with his magnifying glass.

'Fishbreath – is it really you?' he finally gasps. 'But… but it's been years!'

'Fishbreath is the cook aboard my ship, the Black Hound,' says the Captain. 'A fine one too, keeps us all fed and watered.' He grins, patting his stomach.

Fergus reaches over to shake his brother's hand, and when Fishbreath offers him the battered spoon on the end of his arm, Fergus pulls him in for a rather awkward hug. Fishbreath stands stiff, arms tight by his side, his face reddening, and his eyes bulging like he can't breathe.

'I can't believe it,' says Fergus. 'My little brother, after all this time. So, you work for the Captain?'

Fishbreath takes a step backwards and scowls.

'Aye, I have to work for my living, seein' as Pa didn't leave me a big wad of money to buy a huge castle like this one.'

'The high life, it's not all it seems, y'know,' Fergus laments. 'Can have its problems too.'

Fishbreath is about to say something rude, so the Captain butts in quickly.

'I can see that it might be hard,' he says. He gestures towards the far end of the hall, where the feast has erupted into a full-on rumpus.

'You Swamp Squabblers all stink,' goads one clan chief.

'Well, it's a well-known fact that Marsh Muggers are stupid,' another one sneers.

'Least we're not sneaky, like them pilferin'
Peat Plunderers.'

'Or worse still, lily-livered like you Bog
Barbarians. Everyone knows you lot are gutless.
Call yourselves brave? The only thing your
clan is famous for is the prize it got for winning
"Best Kept Bogland Castle" five years ago.'

Fergus looks embarrassed.

'See what I mean?' he says. 'It's not all plain
sailin' round here.'

'Is it always like this?' the Captain asks.

Fergus nods sadly.

'Perils of being the host, I'm afraid. For a start, you've got to expect everyone's going to drink too much grog. Egfart, that brute who told the story about the Ice Pirates, he's the worst. He's Chief of the Swamp Squabblers, an' his clan don't see eye-to-eye with the Marsh Muggers. Then there's the Peat Plunderers – they're so mean they'd fight with their own shadow.'

'But don't you all live on the same boggy island?' I ask.

'Doesn't mean we're all going to get along like a castle on fire. Now come on, Captain, sit down at my table and I'll have someone bring you food and grog. You must be famished an' parched after travellin' all this way.'

After a delicious supper of tasty leftovers from the feast, the Captain asks Fergus about his missing chalice.

'You said in your note it was stolen from the tower,' he says. 'Can you show us where that is?'

We follow Fergus through several large chambers to a twisty spiral staircase. Halfway up the tower, the chief gives us a quick tour of the battlements, showing off a row of large cannons.

'Wow!' says Red. 'They could do some damage.'

Fergus laughs. 'Good job I've never had cause to fire one of 'em yet,' he replies.

My legs are aching
from the climb as we
emerge through a small
wooden door at the top
of the tower. It's dark and
windy outside and a million
stars are sparkling in the skies
above our heads. I look over
the wall, and gasp at the steep
drop to the ground far below.

'You'd need to be a pretty
good climber to scale this
tower from the outside,' I say.

'Yes, but that's what the thief must
have done,' replies Fergus. 'I kept my
precious chalice inside this tower 'cause
I reckoned it would be safe as houses...
Well, castles, if you know what I mean.'

'Do you think it was taken by a Swamp
Squabbler or a Marsh Mugger?' I ask.

'Or a Peat Plunderer,' Red adds.

I am glad, as I had forgotten that name. There sure are a lot of clans in the Boglands.

'To be honest I've no idea,' Fergus shrugs, 'but to do that to me, then to sit downstairs gobbling my roast fowl and guzzling my best grog... Well, it don't bear thinking about. I mean, I know we all have our differences, but at the end of the day we're all still Boglanders.'

'Aye.' The Captain nods. I can tell the case is a mystery to him too, but knowing Captain Watkins, pirate investigator o' the Black Hound, it won't be that way for long.

We go back down the spiral staircase and at the bottom, Fergus sees we are all exhausted.

'I'll show you to your quarters,' he says.

'You're bound to be pooped after such a long day.'

The Captain thanks him, then turns to me. 'Flynn, send a parrot to Briggs telling him all's well, and we'll be staying at the castle till the investigation is over.'

'Aye, Cap'n,' I say.

Fergus gives a half smile at the Captain's confident request. 'Do you think I'll ever see the chalice again, Captain?' he asks.

Watkins slaps him hard on the back. 'No case has beaten us yet, and I don't plan on making yours the first, Fergus,' he replies. 'We'll find it alright. We'll scour every inch of the Boglands if we must. We're pirate investigators and stolen treasure is our speciality.'

CHAPTER FIVE
THE MONSTER'S EYE

The next morning, I wake to the smell of something tasty cooking. Red is already up, which doesn't surprise me. I didn't sleep very well. It took me ages to get used to my hammock when I joined the crew of the Black Hound, but now I really miss it. I get dressed and follow my nose to the large castle kitchen, where I find Fishbreath cooking a hearty breakfast of fried eggs, bacon, bread and butter. A pot of tea bubbles on a stove. There are papers strewn over a long wooden table and Captain Watkins and Fergus are poring over them.

'Good morning.' Fergus nods in my direction. 'Sleep alright?' he asks.

'Not bad, thanks,' I fib, not wanting to hurt Fergus's feelings as he has been so kind.

Red fills me in on the day's plans. 'Today, we're looking for clues in the castle grounds,'

she says, sitting down with a plate piled high with food. She pulls a seat out for me. Watkins comes over to join us and he seems concerned.

'There is very little to go on in this case except a list of all the clan folk who attended the feast before the chalice went missing,' he whispers. 'I wanted to interview the chiefs, but Fergus warned against it until we've got more evidence. They won't take kindly to being questioned without good reason. If they think we're accusing them of something, they might go off on one, especially with a sore head after too much grog.'

Outside, there is a clatter of hooves. I go over to the window and see the chiefs and the clan folk riding off back to their villages.

The castle falls silent.

'Was there talk of the chalice the night it went missing?' Watkins asks Fergus.

He shakes his head. 'Not as far as I can remember.'

'Did you show the chalice to anyone at all? Bring it down for a feast or something?'

'Never. It's too precious to be used. I wouldn't want Egfart or anyone else slobbering all over it.'

After breakfast we leave the castle, with Fergus, Captain Watkins and Fishbreath leading the way.

The brothers are bickering again, so Red and I decide to break away from the group for some peace and quiet.

'Let's split for a while,' I suggest. 'I'm going to explore down by the coast with Red. We can meet up again later.'

Moving off, Red and I start hunting for clues. We walk down the hill away from the castle; the land slopes to the shore, where the Black Hound is anchored in the shallow waters. Suddenly I lose my footing on the steep hill, falling over and rolling downwards, head over heels. My arms flail as I try to stop myself. Behind me, I can hear Red laughing. I fear I might just keep on rolling into the sea – which probably wouldn't be so bad, as Briggs would see me and throw me a rope. But worse than that, I could hit my head on a rock...

Luckily, I land on something soft and furry. It is an enormous ball of packed fur and spit that smells revolting.

Red dashes down the hill, trying not to laugh too hard.

'Flynn! Are you alright?'

'Think so.' I get to my feet.

'Oh, thank goodness. You're lucky you didn't do yourself an injury.'

She helps me brush the icky fur off my clothes.

'What is this stuff?' I ask.

'It's disgusting,' Red chokes.

'Reminds me of the furballs Scratch is always burping up on the Hound, only a hundred times bigger and smellier.'

I hear someone shouting and glance up to see Captain Watkins, Fergus and Fishbreath trudging down the hillside.

'Find anything?' Watkins asks.

'Not unless you call a massive furball a clue?'

Fergus's eyes widen, like he has seen a ghost. 'Couldn't be, could it?' he murmurs, stroking his beard thoughtfully.

'Couldn't be what?'

'Last night, one of the clan chiefs said they reckon Mogdrod is on the prowl again. Swore two of his finest warriors were attacked while they were riding through Bog Forest last week. Only just escaped with their lives.'

'Mogdrod? Who's Mogdrod?' Fishbreath asks, looking nervously over his shoulder.

The colour drains from Fergus's normally rosy cheeks. 'Mogdrod is an ancient creature that's been terrorising folk in the Boglands for centuries. He's a fearsome cat-like beast, with sharp teeth longer than fingers. Only a few of us Boglanders have ever seen him an' lived to tell the tale. I've heard too that Mogdrod has a weakness for shiny things, and to top it all he's a compulsive thief.'

The Captain's eyes light up. 'Could this Mogdrod have stolen your chalice?' he asks.

Fergus shrugs. 'Anything's possible.'

'Looks like your monstrous moggy is our first suspect then,' says Watkins.

I feel a chill run up my spine. Giant cats with teeth as long as fingers... I've never heard of such a thing.

We search along the coast for more clues until a mist starts creeping in from the sea. Visibility is getting worse and worse by the minute. Captain Watkins frowns. 'We're not going to find too many clues in this.'

Fergus nods. 'We should head back to the castle till the fog lifts. Anyway, all this talk of Mogdrod has reminded me there's something I want to show you.'

Back at the castle, we light torches and Fergus leads us down a flight of stone steps and along a narrow, damp corridor to the dungeon. I feel something scurry over my foot and stifle a scream. Even though the Hound is full of rats, I can't stand them!

Soon, we arrive in a dark room, bare except for an old wooden bench and some iron shackles attached to the wall. There is a shelf with something glowing on it.

'Gives me nightmares, so I keep it in the dungeon,' says Fergus.

'Keep what?' Fishbreath asks. 'I always knew you had to have a dark secret in this gloomy castle.'

Fergus reaches up to grab a glass jar with a small, luminous ball inside.

As it rolls around the jar, I notice a coloured circle on one side, with a dark shape at the centre.

I gulp. This is a lot worse than rats.

'It's an eye,' Red gasps.

'Aye,' says the Captain, making a grim joke. Fascinated, he whips out his magnifying glass.

'The eye of Mogdrod,' Fergus breathes. 'It belongs to that creature I told you about.'

'How extraordinary,' mutters Watkins.

'Disgusting,' says Red. 'I bet it smells as bad as that furball thing.'

To my horror the eye fixes me with a grisly
stare, following my every move.

'It's… it's still alive!' I shriek.

'There has to be a kind of dark magic
keeping it alive,' Red gasps.

Fergus frowns. 'It still belongs to Mogdrod,
even though it's no longer connected to his
body. That monster cat keeps his eye alive, and
he's going to be around for some time to come.'

'Why's that?' Red asks.

'Well, just like a cat, Mogdrod has nine lives
and he's almost invincible.'

I can't stop staring at the grisly Eye of Mogdrod.

'Do you think it can see us?' I say, feeling a weird chill. 'It's so creepy that it can still see.'

'Maybe it saw who stole the chalice,' says Red. 'Pity it can't tell us.'

'Maybe Mogdrod came to the castle looking for his eye?' I suggest.

'Then chanced upon the chalice and decided to steal it,' muses the Captain. 'That could be it. Now tell me, Fergus, how did you come by this eerie eye?'

'It was given to me by my cousin, Alfred the Armless,' Fergus explains, launching into a story. 'He's a monk who fought Mogdrod when he was trying to defend his abbey over at Skulleen, one o' the Bogland villages. Mogdrod and his mistress, an old witch called Grethel, had been trying to run off with the abbey's relics when Alfred confronted them.

'There was a big fight and Alfred lost an arm –

but not before he'd gouged out one of the
creature's goggling eyes. Alfred insisted I take
it from him, as he felt it was an evil presence to
have in the abbey.'

'Bet he didn't like the way it looked at him
either,' I say under my breath.

The Captain strokes his chin. 'Hmmm, this is
our first lead and an important one, too,' he says. 'I
think we should follow it up. I propose we make
a start as soon as this mist clears. We'll scour the
whole of this boggy island looking for more clues,
and maybe even pay Alfred the Armless a visit.'

Fergus rolls his eyes. 'No point,' he says.
'My poor old cousin went a bit doolally after

the fight. He wandered off one night, never to be seen again. More like Alfred the Luckless.'

'Sounds like the eye might be cursed,' says Red. She looks excited rather than worried, which is what I feel.

'Don't say that,' says Fergus. 'Maybe that's why I lost my chalice.'

'And maybe that's why I ended up back here with you, big brother,' mutters Fishbreath.

I think about the giant furball and shudder. Did it belong to Mogdrod, the cat-like monster? And had that monster come to the castle to steal the chalice?

We are about to find out.

CHAPTER SIX
QUICKSAND

The mist doesn't lift until the next morning, so we spend another night in lumpy beds in the tower. I am glad it's cleared, as it means we can continue the investigation at last.

'I'd like to come with you again,' Fergus tells the Captain after breakfast. 'Things could get dangerous, especially if the chalice robbery had anything to do with Mogdrod.'

I can tell by the look on Fishbreath's face that he is far from happy at having Fergus in our search party as we set out from the castle.

'Bad enough him tagging along with us yesterday, but here he is again today,' Fishbreath grumbles. 'Got nothing better to do all day, 'cept for sitting on his fancy throne.'

Arthur the parrot squawks, settling on Fishbreath's shoulder. It's almost like he's agreeing with his master.

Visibility is good today and we get to explore much further than before, threading a path through craggy hills and murky woodland.

'Look!' I cry. 'Furballs! There's a trail of them. All fresh too. And see how big they are.'

'I reckon the trail is heading down toward the coast,' says Watkins. 'Let's go that way.' We change direction, following the long line of furballs down to the shore. As we walk, Fergus tries to make small talk with Fishbreath.

'So, what's it like being a pirate?' Fergus asks.

'I told you, I'm not a pirate. I'm a cook,' comes the grumpy reply.

70

'Ex-pirate then. Did you like the letter I sent? Wrote it in my best Piratish, to impress your captain.'

'It was a bit over the top. I could hardly understand a word.'

Fergus laughs, 'That's cos yer not a real pirate, aarrgh!'

Fishbreath sighs deeply and changes the subject.

'So what's it like then, being a chief and having loads of booty?'

'You're not jealous, are you?' Fergus pokes him playfully in the ribs.

'No way. Stuck in a fusty old castle having to eat horrible feast food all day, you must be joking.'

Fergus is offended. 'My feast food's not horrible, it's the best grub in the Boglands,' he protests.

'Don't you two ever stop scrapping?' scolds the Captain. 'Now listen up. The trail goes cold here, and I reckon the tide has washed it away. It could have gone one of two ways from here, so I suggest we split into groups now. Fishbreath, you go west with Flynn and Red. Fergus and I will head east.'

The brothers are happy with this, but Red and I are not so sure. Fishbreath hasn't been much fun to be around since we arrived in the Boglands.

'Good to get a break from my annoying brother,' Fishbreath says as we start out.

72

'You and Fergus sure don't get along,' I say.

He shakes his head. 'If it was up to me, I wouldn't have taken this case. I'd be aboard the Black Hound in the galley, getting lunch ready. I mean, Fergus is a prize idiot. Why would you put the most valuable thing you own in a tower? It's hardly the safest place in the world. He should have hidden his precious chalice in the dungeon with that ugly eye thing. No one would have found it.'

I stop to look down at my shoes, which are covered in muck. 'I have totally the wrong footwear for this,' I say.

'Me too,' Red agrees. 'These buckle boots are ruined.'

'It's getting very swampy all of a sudden,' says Fishbreath. He frowns, his hairy bare feet squelching in the thick black mud. 'Just take it nice and slow and watch yer footing.'

Every step now, I am sinking further into the sludge, making every stride harder to take. Noisier, too, as the sticky mire makes rude farty sounds as we lift our feet.

SQUAWK!

With a flurry of wing beats, Arthur takes to the sky, probably to keep out of my way, as I'm lurching about wildly like a ship in a storm.

'En't happy 'bout this,' Fishbreath grunts. 'This kind of mud can be dangerous.

They call it quicksand out in the Western Isles,
an' it can make a quick meal of yez. I vote we
turn back.'

But this is easier said than done. I try to
turn around, but with both feet stuck firm in the
mud, I end up losing my balance and falling
backwards.

SCHLOOOooOOP!!

I struggle to get up, but mud rises to cover
my legs and waist, like it is swallowing me up.
I sink further and further, until to
my horror I am right inside the
ground itself. Terrified, I hold
my breath and close my eyes as
everything goes black. I wonder
if Red and Fishbreath are sinking
too. Then I feel myself falling into
a deep chasm under the ground.

I can breathe again, but I can't see a thing.
Then I am sliding forward, picking up speed.
I hear a familiar cry and realise Red is down
here too, wherever here is. And I am sure I can
hear Fishbreath groaning somewhere in the
darkness.

'Red! Red, is that you?' I call.

'Flynn, yes it's me. Where are we, and
what's happening?'

'Don't panic!' shouts Fishbreath. 'I think
we're in some sort of mud tunnel. I've heard
about these things, but never fallen into one!
Keep yer arms and legs by yer sides, and let the
mud take us along. Don't resist. Last thing we
want to do is get stuck down here.'

I am scared stiff and don't think I could
move my arms and legs very much, even if I
wanted to. And the smell is terrible, like bad
eggs. I spot a faint chink of light in the distance
growing steadily bigger and my heart leaps.

'I can see daylight,' I yell.

'Me too! Hang on,' Red calls back.

Fishbreath doesn't reply – where is he? Red and I are spewed out of a hole in the hillside, landing with a splash into a shallow pool of muddy water. We are relieved to see Fishbreath already there, wiping mud from his eyes.

'What just happened?' I pant.

'No idea,' gasps Fishbreath. 'It were like a kind of trap. I'm just glad we're all safe now.'

'It stinks!' says Red.

I see something glisten in the sun. It's the glass jar containing the Eye of Mogdrod, floating towards me in the water. Red looks at me accusingly and I make a confession.

'It was me. I stole the eye from the dungeon. Much as I can't stand the thing, I thought it might help us. The Captain said it could be a clue to something. It must have fallen out of my pocket in that mud tunnel.'

Red screws up her face as I fish the jar out of
the mucky pool. 'I can't believe you brought it
with you,' she says.

'Will you carry it in your bag, Red?' I ask.
'I'm afraid if I put it back in my pocket, it might
fall out again.'

'No way, it's disgusting. I don't want to
touch it. Remember what happened to Alfred
the Armless – it might be cursed.'

I shiver, passing her the jar.

'Please!' I say. Red can tell I really mean it.

'I must be mad,' she says, shoving the jar in
her bag.

Fishbreath stands up and points beyond the trees.

'Hey, look over there,' he says.

I follow Fishbreath's gaze to see a tapering tower-like structure, made from grey stone and covered in climbing ivy. It rises above a rocky headland that is being lashed by huge waves.

'That looks like a lighthouse!' Red says. 'But it's abandoned now. Look, there's a lantern room at the top. A bright light would have beamed out from there to warn ships to stay away from these rocks.'

Looking down at the stormy sea, I'm sure the lighthouse must have saved the lives of many pirates back in the day.

'Let's take a closer look,' Fishbreath says, drawing his cutlass. 'Keep yer eyes peeled. We don't know who or what could be lurking inside this place.'

Creeping like burglars, we make our way through the trees toward the old lighthouse. For once, I am glad we have Fishbreath with us, as he looks like he could handle himself well in a fight, with a monster, an Ice Pirate or whoever might cross his path.

There is a heavy wooden door that Fishbreath nods for me to open, as his one good hand is holding a cutlass. The door makes a teeth-clenching scraping sound as I open it, and we all freeze for a moment until Fishbreath waves for us to enter.

'Follow me. Nice and slow, mind.'

I leave the door open to allow some daylight into the fusty hallway.

There seems to be more room inside the lighthouse than you'd think from the outside – it is much bigger than I expected. There are no signs of anyone living here; the walls are bare except for an old, cracked mirror, and the only furniture is a tall wooden cupboard under the stairs. An open door into a smaller room reveals what looks like an old, grubby kitchen with a blackened stove. Not much cooking has been going on here for a while. Trying to make sense of my surroundings, I turn to Red.

'Reckon this old place hasn't been used as a lighthouse for a long time,' I say.

Red agrees. 'Not surprising, when you think about it. Fergus is terrified of Ice Pirates, so he wouldn't want to keep a lighthouse round here. No way he'd want to warn them of any danger – he'd much sooner they dashed their ships on the rocks and sank before they landed.'

There is a sudden commotion in the kitchen.

'Jumpin' jellyfish!' Fishbreath gasps, staring into the cupboard he has just opened. 'Come and see this lot.'

Red and I hurry over to stare at a gleaming pile of silver and gold coins, jewels and goblets. 'Blimey, look at all this booty! There's enough to fill the Captain's old empty chest back on the Hound.'

Red points to a gold cup-like object shoved upside down into a pile of coins. 'Look, it's the chalice!' she says.

The chalice is exactly how Fergus had described it back at the castle: it is cast in bronze, gilded with gold and silver and decorated by carved symbols. It is engraved with the letters FMcS, standing for Fergus McSwaggers.

'No doubt who it belongs to then,' mutters Fishbreath.

'I can't believe we've found it!' Red beams.

'But who took it?' I say.

Fishbreath shrugs. 'Doesn't matter. Fergus is paying us to find it and bring it back to him. All we need to worry about is the big reward he owes us.'

Red is dusting off the chalice to put in her bag when a low growl fills the air. There is a noise like plodding feet on the spiral staircase, getting louder by the second. We are not alone. Someone, or something, is coming down the stairs.

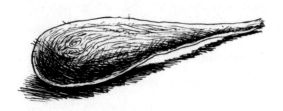

CHAPTER SEVEN
MOGDROD

'We've got to get out of here,' I whisper, grabbing Red by the arm. There is no back door to the lighthouse, so our exit has to be through the kitchen and out the way we came.

We start creeping towards the door when there is another loud, echoing growl. To our horror, a huge cat-like creature bounds down the final few steps of the spiral staircase to block our path, scowling and hissing.

It is as big as a lion, with dark matted fur, ragged ears and cutlass-sharp teeth.

My heart slams in my chest. Taking a step backwards, I see Fishbreath trying to steady his cutlass with a trembling hand.

'Looks like we've got visitors, Kitty,' comes a shrill, crackly voice.

An old woman with long, frizzy grey hair and a pointy nose follows the monstrous cat down the stone steps, pulling her black shawl tight round her shoulders.

More hissing as the creature advances toward us, arching its back.

'Er… look, we don't want any trouble,' says Fishbreath, his voice quivering.

The old woman raises her arm and the feline fiend stops in its tracks. 'Wait, Kitty, let's see what they have to say for themselves.' She turns her attention to us. 'I see you managed to survive my Bog Slide and Peat Plunger.'

'Bog Slide…' I frown, trying to work out what she is on about. But Fishbreath understands at once.

'The traps,' he gasps. 'That was you?'

'Not traps, lures,' she corrects. 'Y'see, I wanted you to come here.'

'Who are you?' Red asks.

'My name is Grethel the Sea Witch.'

It's impossible to ignore the fact that the witch only has one eye. Her working eye is big and goggling. It's also glowing a luminous bright green colour, just like the eye we have hidden away in the jar... I look back at the cat monster, and there's no doubt about it, he's got two eyes and they are both fixed on me with murderous intent. I had thought the fearsome creature must be Mogdrod, but wasn't he supposed to have one eye missing? I put two and two together and make a bold move.

'So, it was you who stole the chalice!' I accuse the witch.

Grethel glances to where Red is still clutching the golden goblet tight to her chest.

'Beautiful, isn't it?' she says. 'Goes perfectly with my collection. I see you haven't brought along the bumbling idiot it belongs to.' Then she begins to cackle. 'Did that brave Fergus McSwaggers tell you he has nightmares about my eye? Can't stand to look at it hardly, that's why he keeps it in that dungeon. What a big baby he is, and him the chief of the fearsome Bog Barbarians... That lot are more like the Bog Baby Scaredy-Cats.' Fishbreath can't suppress a snort of laughter. Grethel gives a smirk in his direction and goes on.

'I watch that Fergus, y'know. He shouts for his mummy, sucks his thumb and blubs like a baby. I know a lot of secrets about his castle too. I might not be able to hear with my missing eye, but I can lip-read.'

Suddenly it all makes sense. Grethel has been watching us too with her gruesome eye; she knows we were searching for Mogdrod and

91

has been waiting here at the lighthouse for us to arrive. But she still hasn't finished her angry tirade.

'Oh, and as for that other fool Alfred the Armless,' she continues. 'Yes, he might've got my eye, but Kitty got his arm and half his relics,

even though he won't admit that bit of the tale. An' he told everyone my eye belonged to Kitty, 'cause a monster's eye makes a much better story to brag about.' She pauses, finally coming to her point. 'Anyway, did you bring it?'

'Bring what?' I ask innocently.

'My eye!'

'No.' My cheeks are burning.

'Liar. I know you did. It fell out of your pocket when you came out of the Bog Slide. I could've cursed you for being so careless. It might've been lost for good. Now give it back.'

'You almost killed us. We could've suffocated in that quicksand or drowned in the swamp.'

'You're as bad as your friend the Baby Bog Chief. You'll hardly drown in a puddle of water.'

Fishbreath wields his cutlass. 'We're taking the chalice back to its rightful owner. Ya got plenty o' treasure here, enough for you and that monster pet of yours. We won't tell a soul about it – you have our word.'

'You'll be doing no such thing. Kitty don't take kindly to anyone touching his sparkly treasure.'

Hissing, Mogdrod thrashes toward us, gnashing his sharp teeth. But above his growls I hear another noise. The sound of heavy boots approaching the lighthouse door, accompanied by gruff voices. A blunt object spins through the air. Then with a blood-curdling howl, Mogdrod collapses in a furry heap on the lighthouse floor, as a heavy club drops by his side.

CHAPTER EIGHT
ICE PIRATES

I've only just got my head round meeting a
fearsome cat-like monster, and now I find
myself up against what looks like a band of
merciless, mud-spattered pirates, only with
white frosty faces and pale blue, staring eyes.

'Ice Pirates. Murderous scoundrels,'
Fishbreath gasps.

'Well, what have we here?' the biggest one
booms, kicking the club across the floor. 'A
dead beast for starters, and by my own fearless

hand. I gave him a whack on the head that sent him out of this world and into the next.'

The band of Ice Pirates say nothing, hardly even cracking a scowl on their frozen faces. A high-pitched shriek pierces the air.

'You killed my Kitty!' Grethel wails and charges bravely at the intruders, teeth and fists bared. But the bulky brute brushes her out of the way like he was swatting a fly.

'Shut up, old hag, or you'll be next.'

'Leave her alone,' I cry, feeling surprisingly sorry for the mad old sea witch. I help Grethel to her feet, and as I look up I recognise the monster slayer.

'Wait a minute, I know you,' I blurt out. 'You're that Egfart the Odorous from the feast at Bog Castle. What are you doing here? And why have you got all these Ice Pirates with you? You hate Ice Pirates – or so you said in that tale you told at the feast!'

A wide toothless grin cuts Egfart's fat face in half.

'Well, maybe you shouldn't believe everything you hear… Looks like you pirate investigators have not only led us to McSwaggers' golden chalice, but a nice little stash of booty to go along with it, eh, men? There's rich pickings for all of us, ya frosty sea dogs.' And he laughs heartily.

'So, you've been following us?' I ask. Seems like everyone has been watching our every move today.

'I knew you'd lead us to the chalice so, yes, I decided to keep a close eye on yez. As for the feast, I made that whole story up about defeating the Ice Pirates. They're on my side – I'm in cahoots with them and have been for ages. A while back, me an' the frosty Ice Pirate Captain had a parley, and we came to a nice little arrangement. He crosses my palm with cold hard silver if I tell 'im the best places to raid up and down these misty shores. Soft targets, I call 'em.'

'Easy pickings,' spits Red. She is furious. 'You dirty rotten turncoat! You'll betray your friends for a bag o' gold!'

'Ye could say that.' Egfart grins. 'Our next target is Fergus's castle, where we last met each other at the feast. This dead monster may have nabbed Fergus's chalice before we got the chance, but there's bound to be lots more booty where that came from.'

'But the Bogland folk are your own people,' I cry, shocked. 'That's the worst form of treachery.'

'The Boglanders aren't my people anymore,' Egfart snarls. 'They're pathetic.'

Even Fishbreath has had enough now.

'You won't get away with this,' he growls. 'The other clans will find out and come after you.'

Egfart laughs. 'Those buffoons are far too busy fighting and bickering among themselves to go for me… That's when they're not gorging on too much food and grog, till they can hardly stand up, let alone fend off an attack from my Ice Pirate pals. Bogland is finished. I realised that a long time ago, so I switched sides… to the winning side!'

He snatches the chalice from Red. 'I'd love to chat, but I have a castle to ransack.'

The pirates draw their cutlasses but Egfart waves a hand dismissively.

'Don't waste blunting yer blades on this feeble lot. Lock 'em in the kitchen and throw away the key.'

I feel a pair of ice-cold hands grab the back of my neck and shove me into the kitchen. I stumble and fall, and Red, Fishbreath and Grethel land on top of me in a sprawling heap. The door slams behind us.

The kitchen is small and gloomy, with one tiny window set high up in the wall.

I sigh. 'Now what?'

Fishbreath tries the door, but it is solid oak – Egfart has locked it from the outside and taken the key. The window is no more than a narrow slit. I am pretty sure even Scratch – the ship's cat on the Hound – couldn't crawl through it.

Fishbreath turns to Grethel. 'You're some kind of witch,' he says. 'So I don't suppose you could cast a spell to open this 'ere door?'

But Grethel is sobbing, shaking her head. 'Kitty, poor Kitty.' She's not going to be much help to anyone in this state.

Beyond the door, there is the sound of clanging metal. 'Listen,' I say. 'They're taking some more treasure, along with Fergus's chalice.'

'Aye, an' they'll be taking a whole lot more once they get to Bog Castle,' says Fishbreath.

He swallows hard. 'I know me and Fergus don't get along, but I've got to help him in his hour of need.'

Fishbreath begins rummaging around the kitchen, pulling food from the cupboards: soggy veg, mouldy bread, stinky cheese and other rotten and forgotten scraps. He mixes them together in a saucepan.

I scratch my head. 'What on earth are you doing, Fishbreath?'

'Never you mind. You and Red are the clever 'uns round 'ere, so just try an' figure out a way to get us out of this kitchen.'

Red and I find a few old rusty keys and try them in the lock but none of them work. It's hopeless.

SQUAWK!

Suddenly, I hear a flurry of wings and a parrot lands on the window ledge up above.

'It's Arthur!' I cry. Fishbreath's trusty mascot. But Fishbreath is so busy with whatever he is up to, he doesn't even notice.

'Could Arthur fly round to the lighthouse entrance and try to find the key?'

Red sighs. 'Egfart has probably thrown it away or taken it with him.'

My mind races and I quickly come up with a plan. 'OK, so look, maybe we are stuck here for a while, but at least there's a way we can get word to Captain Watkins and Fergus, to warn them of the Ice Pirate attack.'

Red looks up at the parrot and smiles. 'Great idea!' she says.

I write a note telling our pirate investigator friends to go straight back to Bog Castle, and if there's time, to round up some Marsh Muggers or Peat Plunderers along the way.

The more the merrier. Meanwhile, Red whistles to Arthur, who flies down from the window ledge and lands on her shoulder. She fixes my note to his scaly leg.

'Off you fly back to the Captain!' she coos, and he squawks in reply, flapping upwards and out through the window.

Fishbreath is still busy in the kitchen. He has even enlisted the help of a snivelling Grethel to help him mix his ingredients.

'Phew! What's that smell, Fishbreath?' I ask, coughing. 'It's disgusting.'

'It's a stink bomb,' he replies with a smirk. 'I'm going to bottle it. We can use it to fend off that toe-rag Egfart.

But it's still going to be getting out of here that's the problem.'

'The smell might kill us before we get out,' I splutter. Fishbreath screws the lid of the bottle shut, just before I almost pass out with the stench.

Grethel helps Fishbreath put the bottled potion under his big, puffy chef hat and as she does, I hear something beyond the door. It sounds like a growl. Weirdly, Grethel claps her hands together, a big grin lighting up her wrinkled face.

'Thank goodness!' she cries. 'Er, you might want to move away from the door.'

'Why? What is it? What's out there?'

The cupboards judder with a loud thud as something slams into the door.

'Red, get out of the way!' I yell.

'What...Why?'

'Just do it!'

108

All of a sudden, the door is ripped from its hinges, to land flat on the kitchen floor. It doesn't take a pirate investigator to work out that if Red had still been standing there, she would have been squished flatter than one of Fishbreath's hardtack biscuits.

When the dust settles, Mogdrod stands silhouetted in the doorway, looking very alive and very angry.

CHAPTER NINE
THE DEAL

'Kitty!' the old witch cries gleefully.

'How is he still alive?' I ask, astonished.

'Because he's got nine lives, like all cats do, and I'm happy to say that silly old me can't count,' she replies. 'I was sure he was gone for good that time.'

Mogdrod looms toward us, drooling from his needle-like fangs. I notice Fishbreath reach for the stink bomb he has been hiding under his hat.

'Tell him to back off!' I yell at Grethel.

'Look, in case you haven't realised, we're not the enemy here. We don't even have the chalice – Egfart's got it. And you're forgetting, we do have something you actually want.'

Red and Fishbreath stare at me as I grab Red's bag and take out the glass jar. Gingerly, I unscrew the lid and pluck out the luminous eye, resting it on my palm. It feels soft and wobbly like jelly, and smells disgusting.

'If you let your Kitty hurt any of us, I swear I'll squish your eye to a pulp.'

Grethel clenches her fists. 'Give it back, you sneaky little sea rat.'

'On one condition. Well, two, actually,' I reply.
'First, you call off your pet monster and secondly,
help us and the crew of our ship fight Egfart the
traitor and his greedy gang of Ice Pirates.'

'What? You're crazier than me, boy!' she
gasps. 'You don't stand a chance against
those bloodthirsty maniacs.'

'We can try at least. They're heading for Bog
Castle right now, and we have to help Fergus
and the Bog Barbarians defend their property.'

'You'll get your treasure back,' Red promises. 'Plus the Ice Pirates will have a ton of lovely booty on their ship, which is another good reason to chase them down.'

Grethel pauses for a moment, stroking her whiskery chin. Mogdrod stands hissing, his gaze darting between each of us and his crazy mistress. But when he starts edging toward me again, I give the eye a firm squeeze.

'Stop!' Grethel screams, holding her head in her hands. 'OK. OK, I'll do it. Leave them alone, Kitty. Just don't do that again, boy. It's like someone is squashing my brain.'

Mogdrod lets out a sort of a whimpering growl, then lies down reluctantly.

I turn my attention back to Grethel.

'You'll help us then?' I ask.

She nods. 'We'll help each other. Not because I've gone all soft, mind, but because we've got more chance of getting back my booty if we all join forces. Did you say there are more of you pirate investigators?'

'A whole ship of 'em, under the fearless command of Captain Watkins, the best sailor in the Seven Seas. If anyone can defeat the Ice Pirates, he can.'

'Then what are we waiting for?' asks Red.

'There is just one small thing,' Grethel says. She puts out her hand.

'Of course.' I hand her the eye, which she promptly pops back into her head.

'Ha ha!' she cackles. 'It feels so good to be able to see properly again.' She looks Fishbreath up and down. 'Hmmm. You're even more handsome than I thought, pirate boy.'

Fishbreath blushes.

'Er… I think we should get going,' he says quickly.

We set off for Bog Castle. Grethel leads the way, insisting that Fishbreath sticks close behind her. As we walk uphill, she slips on the muddy path, falling backwards into Fishbreath's arms. Mogdrod hisses loudly in his face. Anyone would think he was jealous of the old sea dog.

'Enough of that, Kitty,' scolds Grethel, looking a bit pink.

The ground is getting squelchier, and I smell the same rotten smell we noticed on our way to the lighthouse.

'We're not going to fall into your Peat Plunger again, are we?' I ask Grethel anxiously.

She grins. 'Don't worry, you're safe enough. I know a shortcut through the hills. Quick, let's hurry up.'

Soon we reach the brow of the hill. An icy wind whips in from the sea and I feel my cheeks sting. Down below, a low mist skirts the coastline.

'Look, there's a ship in the bay!' Red cries.

'It's the Hound,' says
Fishbreath. 'The Captain must
have got a message to the crew.
They've come to help us.'

A cold fear grips me as
I notice the flag on top of
the main mast. It's a frosty skull,
criss-crossed with icicles.

'That's not the Hound,' I say, my voice
trembling. 'That's an Ice Pirate ship!'

CHAPTER TEN
FIRE IN THE HOLE

Red and I stare at each other, a look of horror on our faces. What kind of low-life monster is Egfart? He hasn't wasted a minute in leading the merciless Ice Pirates to ransack Fergus's castle, and after that probably taking them further inland to loot some of the defenceless Bogland villages.

My heart is hammering. Peering through the mist, I can see there are two ships in the bay – the first is the Ice Pirate ship, and

the second is the Black Hound. Red takes a
spyglass out of her bag and trains it on the
enemy ship.

'It's sailing straight for the Hound!' she
says. 'There are Ice Pirates hanging from the
rigging – I can just make out their white locks
blowing in the wind. It looks like a ship full
of bloodthirsty ghouls.'

We take cover in some thick bushes. I scan the shore and notice a jolly boat hauled up on the beach. Another is making its way to the shore, packed full of Ice Pirates.

The Ice Pirate ship fires a bolt of solid ice that rips through the Hound's rigging, tearing the main sail.

'The Black Hound is under ice attack!' I cry.

'That's your ship?' Grethel says scornfully. 'What kind of name is the Black Hound? You should have called it the Black Kitty. My Mogdrod hates hounds.' She gives her giant pet a pat on the head.

Fishbreath sighs. 'There are more important things to worry about than the name of our ship,' he complains. 'Can't you see the Hound is in serious danger?'

Grethel looks hurt. 'No need to be cheeky. I can see twice as well now as I could before.'

'We've got to help!' Red says.

'But we need a plan,' I sigh, in despair.

There is a flash of fire from the deck of the Hound, and in a puff of smoke, a cannonball streaks towards the Ice Pirate ship.

'Go on, Hudson,' Red yells. 'Give 'em as good as you get!'

Grethel shakes her fist at the Ice Pirates. 'Those rotten robbers have got my booty. Why are we hiding in these stupid bushes? Let's go and fight them!'

Mogdrod roars, as though like Grethel, he can't wait to pounce on them.

'Wait!' I say. 'How many lives did you say Mogdrod's got left, Grethel?'

'I've lost count. Not many.'

'Well, just think about it. If we send him to fight that lot, he'll use his lives up in no time. There are too many of them.' I point to the castle tower. 'I've got a better idea, but I need to get up to that parapet. There's a cannon up there I could use to fire at the Ice Pirates. If I can somehow bombard their ship, then they'll have to flee.'

Fishbreath grabs Red's spyglass and peers through it toward the castle.

'The guards have been tied up,' he says. 'That means the Ice Pirates must have breached the castle and they'll be inside now. Who's to say they aren't already up in the tower?'

'It's a chance I have to take,' I reply, frowning. 'But I reckon they'll be too busy looking for loot to bother with going up there. Grethel, do you think Mogdrod could climb up the tower again, only with me on his back this time?'

Grethel nods. 'He'll do whatever I ask him to do.' She smiles a toothless grin at Fishbreath. Flustered, Fishbreath takes off his hat and hands me the stink bomb he made at the lighthouse.

'Here, take this with you. It might buy you time if you run into bad company up there.'

At Grethel's instruction, Mogdrod crouches down low, tail between his legs. I climb onto his back, clinging to a few clumps of tangled fur. Then, without warning, we're off. He chases over to the castle and effortlessly begins to climb the outside walls of the tower. I close my eyes, too afraid to look, and quickly stop worrying about holding on to his fur too tightly. It was either that, or fall back down to the ground, probably breaking every bone in my body.

At the top, I clamber off Mogdrod and rush over to a large barrel to grab what I need. But my heart sinks.

'There's plenty of gunpowder in here, but no cannonballs,' I say to Mogdrod. 'Now, what are we going to do?'

Mogdrod's face contorts as he starts retching. Seconds later he spews up a cannonball-sized furball, tightly packed and hard as rock.

'Excellent job, Kitty.' I grin.

I hurry over to load the cannon. Lucky that back on the Hound, Red had showed me how to fire a cannon, so I can remember what to do.

Loading the muzzle, I light the touch hole.

'Stand back, Mogdrod,' I yell. 'Fire in the hole!'

My heart leaps as I watch the giant hairball streak through the sky and crash into the Ice Pirate ship, splintering the foresail to smithereens.

'Direct hit, Mogdrod! Quick, let's reload.'

Mogdrod retches up another hairball, even stinkier than the first. But then I hear a familiar voice call out.

'Well, look who it is. Our junior pirate investigator. Reckon you can take on the Ice Pirates single-handed?'

I turn round as Egfart bursts out laughing.

'Got guts, I'll say that for you. More than your friends the Bog Barbarians.'

'Back off, Egfart, or I'll set Mogdrod on you.'

'Ah, that mangy old fleabag. I wondered how you lot managed to escape from the

132

lighthouse, but then I remembered him. He really does have more lives than a cat. But he won't after I've finished with him. You'll both be wishing you'd stayed locked up in that smelly lighthouse kitchen.'

'You'll never get away with this, Egfart,' I threaten. 'The Ice Pirate ship is no match for the Black Hound. You should go before they sink it to the bottom of the Frozen Sea.'

He laughs again. 'Other way round, I'd say. The hull of your ship has so many holes, it looks like a lump of cheese. But actually, I'm sort of glad I found you. It was you who led me to the last stash of booty, so now you're going to show me where McSwaggers has hidden the rest of his gold.'

Just then I hear a loud horn. It sounds like it's coming from the Ice Pirate ship.

I look over the parapet.

'I think you should probably see this, Egfart. Looks like your Ice Pirate pals have had enough. That horn is a call to raise anchor. The jolly boat has turned around and is heading back to the ship. Told you they were no match for the Hound.'

'Lying snake. Ice Pirates are like Swamp
Squabblers, they never retreat. You really are
beginning to annoy me, y'know.' Raising his
spear, he waves it in the air. 'Take me to the
booty or I'll run yez through like a slab o' soft
butter!' he scowls.

CHAPTER ELEVEN
RETREAT

Egfart lunges at me across the parapet, jabbing with his spear. Suddenly I remember Fishbreath's stink bomb and take it out of my pocket. I toss it at Egfart's feet and it smashes, exploding in a foul cloud that spreads over the battlements like Bogland mist. Egfart stops in his tracks and falls to his knees, coughing and retching. Prepared for this, I have already covered my nose and mouth with my neckerchief.

'Quick, Mogdrod!' I cry, my words muffled.
'We've got to climb back down and find
out what's going on.' I'd like to have fired
off another shot, but it looks like there is no
need. The Ice Pirate ship seems to be getting
ready to sail and another jolly boat is rowing
frantically away from the shore.

I jump onto Mogdrod's back, clinging on
for dear life as he clambers down the side of
the tower. My heart leaps for joy when I see
a line of warriors, swords and spears in hand,
marching over the brow of the hill.

'Boglanders!' I gasp. 'They've come.'

We reach the ground and Mogdrod shakes me off, bounding back to Grethel and the others who are still hiding down in the bushes. At this moment, Egfart and the Ice Pirate Captain stumble out of the castle entrance. I take cover under the drawbridge. Egfart is still hacking and coughing from the effects of Fishbreath's stink bomb. The colour drains from their faces as they spot the army of Bog Barbarians on the horizon.

'So that's why they've blown the horn for retreat,' Egfart exclaims, sounding disgusted.

'There are too many of them,' says the Ice Pirate Captain. 'Back to the jolly boats, lads!' he yells to his crew, glancing worriedly up the hill at the advancing attackers.

Ice Pirates pour out of the castle, carrying armfuls of treasure. They scramble down the hill, dropping some of the loot in their rush to get to the boats.

'This is all your fault, Egfart,' fumes the Ice Pirate Captain. 'If we hadn't gone to find McSwaggers' golden chalice, we would have looted his entire castle by now. And it was your idea to lock the old hag and the others in the kitchen, when we should have finished them off. You let them get away, so they could send out a warning to their friends.'

'But that chalice is the most prized piece of booty in all the Seven Seas,' argues Egfart. 'Anyway, why are we running? Stay and fight. I know we're outnumbered, but they're just a bunch of softies. We can easily defeat them.'

'If you're so sure about that, you stay. Oh, and you can forget about helping us anymore. In future, we'll plan our own raids.'

'What! But what about the parley? We had a deal!'

'The deal's off.'

Egfart raises his big boulder fists. 'You're just as bad as they are! Not so much cold-hearted killers as soft-headed cowards. You frosty fools! You icy idiots! No one gets the better of Egfart the Odorous! And if the deal is off, then I'll be having my cut of the booty.'

Egfart whacks the Ice Pirate Captain over the head with his spear, snatching his sack of treasure, then starts blundering down the hill.

I see that he is fleeing in the direction of the bushes where Mogdrod and the others are hiding. I yell down to them from my hiding place.

'Egfart's getting away and he's got the chalice!'

Mogdrod steps out from the bushes to confront Egfart, but the chief lunges back with his spear, yelling madly. In a lightning move, Mogdrod shoots out a huge paw, batting the spear from Egfart's hand like he is swatting a fly. And one more swipe sends Egfart flying. He lands in a heap at Fishbreath's feet, and the cook stamps on his shoulder, drawing his cutlass.

Coming down the hill, Captain Watkins is leading the Bog army, with Fergus by his side.

'Quick march!' Watkins orders, heading the Boglanders towards the coast. I realise

he is making sure the Ice Pirates don't have
any second thoughts about their retreat. The
Captain takes one last look up at Bog Castle
and spots me by the drawbridge. He waves
at me to come down and join them.

As I approach he claps me on the back.
'Ya done well, Flynn. All o' yez did. The
parrot idea worked a treat. Kept us all in the
loop. Yer takin' to this pirate investigating
like a shark to water.'

Fergus smiles. 'Aye, we were heading for
the villages when the parrot delivered your
message to the Captain here,' he says. 'That
was a proper bit of genius on your part, lad.
You saved my castle from being ransacked.'

'I'm glad it worked out,' I say, swelling with
pride. 'And it's good to see the backs of those
scurvy Ice Pirates.' A thought occurs to me.

'Come with me,' I say to Fergus.

We split off from Watkins and the Bogland army, hurrying over to where Fishbreath is standing over a furious-looking Egfart.

Fergus scowls at him, shaking his head. 'You're a disgrace, Egfart,' he says. 'You spouted nothing but lies at my feast. You're a traitor and you've brought shame on yer tribe.'

'Yer all a bunch of wimps,' Egfart snarls, struggling to break free. 'You haven't heard the last of the Ice Pirates. They'll be back, and so will I.'

'Where's my chalice, Egfart?' Fergus demands, using his spear to rummage through the sack of spilled booty that is strewn over the ground.

Egfart points to the Ice Pirate Captain as he zig-zags down to the coast. They watch as he wades into the sea, making for the last jolly boat.

'He took your precious goblet. Ya got no chance o' getting it back now,' Egfart jeers.

But I'm not so sure. I spot something shiny sticking out of Egfart's furry tunic. I crouch down to pull free the beautiful golden cup.

'Nice try, Egfart.' I smile. 'You're a liar to the last. You really don't know when to give up, do you?'

CHAPTER TWELVE
BACK ABOARD THE HOUND

That evening, Captain Watkins invites Fergus as guest of honour to a special supper aboard the battered but not beaten Black Hound. I help Briggs bring up more tables from the mess to the Captain's cabin and we shove them together to make a long banqueting table. It is good to see the rest of the crew again.

'Good job, Flynn.' Fergus grins. 'Be thinking I'm back in the Great Hall at this rate.'

'What about Egfart? What's going to happen to him?' I ask.

'He's enjoying his first night in the dungeon. He'll stay there a while until we decide to return him to his own clan. It'll be up to them to work out how to punish him, but one thing's for sure: the Swamp Squabblers will be looking for a new chief.'

The door opens and a small, hooded figure carrying two large jugs of grog totters in, mumbling to herself.

'Grethel?' I gasp. 'What are you doing here?'

'Ah, yes, before we get started, I have some news,' the Captain announces. 'I would like to introduce you all to one of our newest crew members, Grethel. She's going to be giving Fishbreath a hand in the kitchen and helping Hudson with stores and supplies for a while.'

Setting the grog on the table, Grethel flashes me a toothless grin.

'Why not, eh?' she says. 'I enjoyed helping you out and I've got a bit of a soft spot for your handsome cook. Besides, I'm partial to shiny things, so helping you find lost treasure on your investigations might be right up my street.'

I shoot a glance at Fishbreath, who looks mortified.

'But what about Mogdrod?' I ask.

The Captain smiles. 'Never seen anyone climb the rigging quite like Mogdrod, so he'll be keeping lookout for us. He'll come in handy if we ever run into a spot of bother again. As you know, the Seven Seas can be deadly if you don't have yer wits about you, and a good cutlass. Our Mogdrod has a paw an' a jaw full o' cutlasses.'

'He's already done a great job mending the sails that were damaged by the Ice Pirate attack,' Hudson points out.

'Splendid. So, what's the latest damage report, Hudson?'

'Nothing that'll stop us putting out to sea again first thing in the morning.'

I feel something furry rub against my shin and look under the table to find Scratch on the prowl. I give her a rub between the ears.

'You know there's one thing Mogdrod can't do, and that's chase rats off this ship,' I say. 'He's far too big and blundering for that. So, our Scratch is still the number one rat-catcher round here. And she's got a big brother on board now, just like Fishbreath!' Scratch looks at me with her one eye and I'm sure she gives me a knowing wink, as if to say she can outwit her big brother any day of the week.

Fishbreath fetches a trayful of food, setting down roast hog, bread, vegetables and fruit on the table.

'Don't be thinking you'll get all this once we're back at sea.' He grins. 'Most o' this grub and grog came by kind donation of the Bog Castle kitchen.'

'It's the least I could do,' Fergus beams,
admiring his golden chalice, which has pride
of place in the centre of the table.
'I'm thankful to all of you for the safe return
of my treasure, not to mention for seeing off
the Ice Pirates and exposing Egfart for the
despicable traitor he is.'

Fergus walks around the table, pouring the grog into cups. 'And at my next feast, I'm going to put it to the other clan chiefs that we all try to pull together as Boglanders, so we can stop our stupid squabbling. As we've seen, the threat from the Ice Pirates is real, and we need to pay more attention to it. The more we stick together, the better chance we have of fending them off.'

Fishbreath, Red and I are tucking into
the feast when Fergus sits down beside us,
putting a hand on his brother's shoulder.

'I've been thinking, Fishbreath, I could
really use you here,' he says. 'I noticed how
you dealt with Egfart today – it was brilliant.
For the first time, I realised there's Bog
Barbarian in you, hidden behind all your
piratey ways. Listen, I've decided to give you
part of my castle.'

Fishbreath almost chokes on a mouthful
of grub.

'What?' he splutters.

Fergus takes out a scroll of paper. He's clearly not joking.

'Here are the castle deeds. I'm willing to sign the tower over to you right now.'

Fishbreath reads the scroll, his bushy eyebrows raised, then smiles and pushes it back across the table.

'Thanks, big brother, but no thanks.
Maybe there's some Bog Barbarian in me,
but there's a lot more pirate investigator.
Sailing on the Black Hound and the open sea
is where I want to be, along with these two
scallywags, eh?' He grins at me and Red.

   'Aye, Fishbreath,' says Red,
 looking chuffed. 'We'd miss you
if you ever left.''

'It's your grub that keeps us all going,'
I add. 'We'd be lost without you.'

Fishbreath takes a bite out of a big, juicy
rib, then grins.

'Got to admit it though, Fergus, your feast
grub maybe en't too bad after all.'

* * *

After the feast, Red and I make our way
across the main deck to return to our
hammocks for the night.

'Reckon if I ate one more sausage I'd
burst,' Red says, putting her first foot on the
ladder down to the hold.

'It's so good to be back on board again,' I
say. 'And it's great that Grethel and Mogdrod
have joined the crew.'

Red smiles. 'Grethel's taken me under her
wing,' she says. 'S'funny, she reminds me of the
mad old crone I worked for before I ran away to
sea – guess they're both witches. Our Grethel's
much nicer though. She's offered to teach me to
read, and I might just take her up on it.'

I laugh. 'You'll be the first to read about
our next case when it flies in by parrot,' I say.
Suddenly there is a loud throbbing noise.
'Sshh, did you hear that?' I whisper.

'Hear what?' says Red, stopping still.

'Sounds like… snoring.'

'Wait, that's not snoring...'

I look up the main mast and see Mogdrod's paws dangling over the edge of the crow's nest. He is purring very loudly, obviously content with his new job as pirate investigator and chief rigger.

'Hey, that's my bed up there… sometimes,' Red laughs.

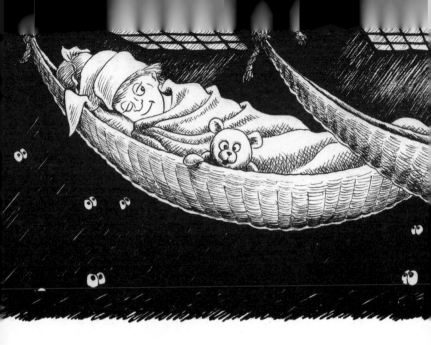

Below deck in the ship's sleeping quarters, we climb into our hammocks. I lie back, staring at the wooden rafters. I'm pretty sure I can still hear Mogdrod purring, way up above our heads. It's kind of reassuring, like having a giant guard dog on duty, only in this case, it's the biggest cat on the Seven Seas.

'Aren't you glad, Red, that we don't have

to spend another night in that draughty old tower?' I ask.

No answer.

I peer out of my hammock, only to see that Red is already out for the count.

'Beat me to it, as usual,' I say, then lie back in my hammock, waiting for the gentle waves to rock me to sleep.

Look out for Book Three:
THE GHOST OF SCARLETBEARD

The Countess of Bohemia's jewels have been stolen by
a ghost. Not just any old ghost, but the ghost of Captain
Scarletbeard, the scariest pirate who ever lived!

Flynn and the crew of the Black Hound descend
the murky depths to Davy Jones's Locker, where
they uncover a ghoulish plot that threatens
the survival of the Seven Seas…